HILDA HEN'S SEARCH

For Lucy

MARY WORMELL

HILDA HEN'S SEARCH

HARCOURT BRACE & COMPANY

San Diego   New York   London

Printed in Hong Kong

Hilda Hen wanted to lay some eggs,
so off she went to the henhouse.

But when she got there, all the nests were full.
  "No room, sorry," squawked the hens.
  "Never mind, I can't nest here," sighed Hilda.
"It's much too busy. I shall just have to find
somewhere else."

And off she went.

"Now, this looks fine," clucked Hilda.
She started to arrange the straw, when . . .

"Meow, meow," mewed the kittens.
"Dear me, I can't nest here!" cried Hilda.
"It's much too scratchy. I shall just have to
find somewhere else."

And off she went.

"Ah, this looks cozy," clucked Hilda.
She started to settle down, when . . .

"Ding, ding," rang the bell.

"My goodness, I can't nest here!" cried Hilda. "It's much too noisy. I shall just have to find somewhere else."

And off she went.

"Now, this looks comfy," clucked Hilda.
She started to doze off, when . . .

"Flap, flap," went the laundry.
   "Oh, no, I can't nest here!" cried Hilda.
"It's much too windy. I shall just have to
find somewhere else."

And off she went.

"Yes, this looks better," clucked Hilda.
She was feeling pleased, when . . .

"Munch, munch," chewed the horse.
"Help, I can't nest here!" cried Hilda.
"It's much too risky. I shall just have to
find somewhere else."

And off she went.

"Now, this looks lovely," clucked Hilda.
"I wonder if this will be the right place?"
She waited and waited . . .

but no one came. So Hilda Hen laid her eggs in peace, and hatched them.

"I think I chose the best place of all,"
clucked Hilda happily.

And everyone agreed.

Requests for permission to make copies of any part
of the work should be mailed to: Permissions Department,
Harcourt Brace & Company, 6277 Sea Harbor Drive,
Orlando, Florida 32887-6777.

Library of Congress Cataloging-in-Publication Data
Wormell, Mary.
Hilda Hen's search/by Mary Wormell. — 1st U.S. ed.
p.   cm.
Summary: A mother hen tries several different places
before she finds the right spot to lay and hatch her eggs.
ISBN 0-15-200069-0
[1. Chickens—Fiction.]   I. Title.
PZ7.W88774Hi   1994
[E]—dc20   93-20986

A B C D E